T...
bel...

CW00539023

The
Water Fairies

Illustrated by

Margaret W. Tarrant

Original poetry by

Marion St. John Webb

Series Editor

Fiona Waters

·MARGARET TARRANT'S·
FAIRIES & FLOWERS

First published in this format in 2003 by
The Medici Society Ltd
Grafton House, Hyde Estate Road, London NW9 6JZ

Copyright © The Medici Society Ltd 2003 / 1925

First published as The Pond Fairies in 1925 by The Medici Society Ltd
1 3 5 7 9 10 8 6 4 2

The rights of Margaret Tarrant and Marion St John Webb to be identified
as the Illustrator and Author of this work have been asserted by them in
accordance with the Copyright, Design and Patents Act 1988.

A catalogue record for this book is available from the British Library.

ISBN 0 85503 252 9

Margaret Tarrant's original artworks have been rescanned for this re-designed edition.

Designed by Tony Potter Publishing Ltd

Printed in Singapore

The
Water Fairies

Contents

Among the Tadpoles ...   9

The Fairy Omnibus ...   15

The Tale of a Toad ...   21

The Fairy without any Wings ... 27

Raindrops ...   33

Seeing Fairies ...   39

Margaret Winifred Tarrant ...   44

Of course, it isn't every pond
That has a fairy in it,
But I can show you one I've found
If you can spare a minute.

Among the Tadpoles

"The little pond," I thought,
"Is full of stars tonight,"
And I looked again to see
The tiny gleams of light.
They winked so brightly up to me,
Like friendly, watching eyes.
But then I lifted up my head
And I saw just cloudy skies . . .
There were no stars!

"The little pond," I thought,
"Is full of dreams tonight.
And all those dreams are mine."
The tiny little gleams of light
Winked brightly up at me.
And then, suddenly, I knew
That they were fairy eyes!
And all my dreams came true . . .
They were not stars!

The best of dreams the little pond may give,
For here among the tadpoles, fairies live!

The Fairy Omnibus

A newt came swimming by this way
    And said he was happy to be
Our local bus, one every day
From the boot to the little bent tree.

You wait at the bottom, beside the old boot
When you want to get on to the bus.
There's always a scramble, and quite a to-do,
And everyone makes such a fuss.

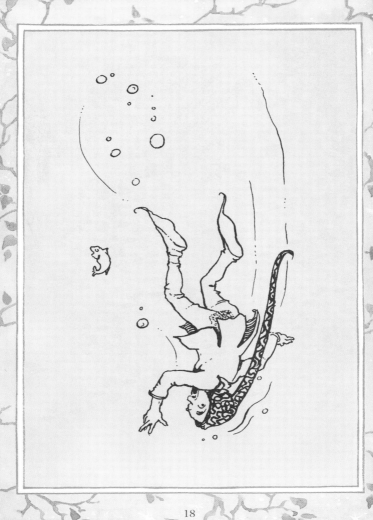

A bit of green weed is the fare,
As the fairies climb on to the newt.
But they are lucky to get where they want,
They usually fall off en route!
Well, they need to hold firm,
And not wriggle and squirm
For the newt's very slippery indeed!
Now he's made a new suit,
Just right for a newt,
From the bus fares of shiny green weed!

Margaret W Tarrant

The Tale of a Toad

The toad had never seen a fairy,
So, of course, he used to say,
"I don't believe in fairies.
There are no such things today!"

One day he went walking
Across the marsh and beyond.
He found a daisy meadow,
With a little hidden pond.

And over all the water
Fairies darted here and there.
The toad sat silent, watching,
Then asked them what they were.

They told him they were fairies.
But he gave a croak and said,
"There are no fairies living,
All the fairies now are dead!"

"You must be some new insect."
And he gave another croak.
Then he picked himself some flowers.
"Fairies! What a silly joke!"

The fairies started laughing:
"You may call us what you will.
It really doesn't matter,
There are plenty fairies still!"

Although he'd seen the fairies
As the toad went home that day,
"I've seen some queer new insects,"
His neighbours heard him say.

Now, tell me why do you suppose
Toad won't believe in fairies
When they're right before his nose?

The Fairy without any Wings

"What is the use of being a fairy
        When I haven't any wings?"
That is the song one little fairy
Wearily and sadly sings.
"What is the use of being a fairy,
When of the clouds I'm fond?
But I simply can't fly,
Though I try and try?
And I hate to live in a pond!"

"Use what you've got," says the
  Pond-lily Fairy.
"Think of the thousands of things,
All of them kind and all of them
  helpful,
That you can do without any wings!
For a fairy who tries
Could enchant butterflies
So they'll give you a ride,
Over far and wide.

And that is the answer
For all wingless things.
If they've none of their own,
They must borrow some wings!

Raindrops

There's a little band of fairies
Who care for all the flowers
That grow upon the pond top.
And during sunny hours
The dainty water-crowfoot
Will spread its petals out,
And all the little fairies come
To dance around about.

The crowfoot loves the sunshine,
But rain does not appeal.
The raindrops' pitter-patter
It does not like to feel.
So when the rain is starting,
The anxious fairies cry:
"Come quickly underneath, my dears,
And from the rain keep dry!"

They pull the crowfoot under,
And hide it from the rain.
Beneath the pond they hold it
Till sunshine comes again.
And then they lift it gently,
It spreads its petals out,
And all the little fairies come
And dance around about.

Seeing Fairies

There are many ways of seeing fairies:
    Some folk simply stand and call!
Some folk find a different way
And so see them every day,
And some have never found a way at all.

An easy way upon the pond
Is shown to us by the duck.
He swims around a little while,
And then he tries his luck
By swiftly standing on his head!
For now he's found that he
Can always find a fairy when
He's upside down, you see.
But, right way up, he'll peer and stare,
And not see fairies anywhere!

There are many ways of seeing fairies:
You can climb the nearest wall!
Some folk try a different way
And so see them every day,
But some have never found a way at all!

Margaret Winifred Tarrant (1888 - 1959)

'Every time a child says,' " I don't believe in fairies," ' warned Peter Pan, 'there is a little fairy somewhere that falls down dead.' By her paintings Margaret Tarrant did as much to stop this happening as J M Barrie did by his writings.

Born in London in 1888, the only child of artist Percy Tarrant and his wife Sarah, Margaret excelled at art from an early age, and she was only 19 when she received her first, very prestigious, commission, from J M Dent & Sons: to illustrate Charles Kingsley's much-loved children's classic, *The Water Babies*, which was first published in 1863.

Her delicate, charming pictures matched the spirit of the story perfectly and earned her a string of new commissions: *Nursery Rhymes* (1914 and 1923), *Alice in Wonderland* (1916) and *Hans Andersen's Fairy Tales* (1917) for Ward Lock & Co., plus postcards for Oxford University Press.

She illustrated some 20 books for George G. Harrap & Co. between 1915 and 1929, but an even more important publishing relationship began in 1920, when she completed her first pieces for The Medici Society. This was to prove a long and fruitful connection, resulting in most of her best-known work. In the 1920s, for example, she illustrated this highly successful series of fairy books for the company, written by the poet and author Marion St John Webb. Her picture of Peter's Friends, inspired by J M Barrie's *Peter Pan* stories and the statue in Kensington Gardens, proved so popular when it appeared in 1921 that it had to be reproduced many times.

During her life Margaret Tarrant tackled a wide range of subjects and won special acclaim for those, such as *All Things Wise and Wonderful,* with a religious theme. But her forte was fairies. She would sketch meticulously from life to capture the likeness of a child or plant, then compose her pictures by arranging the subjects in imaginary settings, infusing them with a distinctive otherworldly quality. Her fairies have a unique fluidity and balletic grace that expressed her delight in the free-flowing dance invented by Isadora Duncan.

Much missed when she died in 1959, Margaret Tarrant left a lasting legacy in charming pictures that seem as fresh today as the day they were painted, and still enchant new generations with their glimpses into a secret fairy world.

The new edition

There are 12 beautiful fairy books by Margaret Tarrant, originally published between 1923 - 1928. The re-designed edition is now available to collect as a set, with modern scanning methods used to bring out the exquisite detail of the original paintings and drawings.

WATER FAIRIES — WATER FAIRIES

TWILIGHT FAIRIES — TWILIGHT FAIRIES

WEATHER FAIRIES — WEATHER FAIRIES

ORCHARD FAIRIES — ORCHARD FAIRIES

WILD FRUIT FAIRIES — WILD FRUIT FAIRIES

INSECT FAIRIES — INSECT FAIRIES

HOUSE FAIRIES — HOUSE FAIRIES

FOREST FAIRIES — FOREST FAIRIES

SEED FAIRIES — SEED FAIRIES

SEASHORE FAIRIES — SEASHORE FAIRIES

FLOWER FAIRIES — FLOWER FAIRIES

HEATH FAIRIES — HEATH FAIRIES

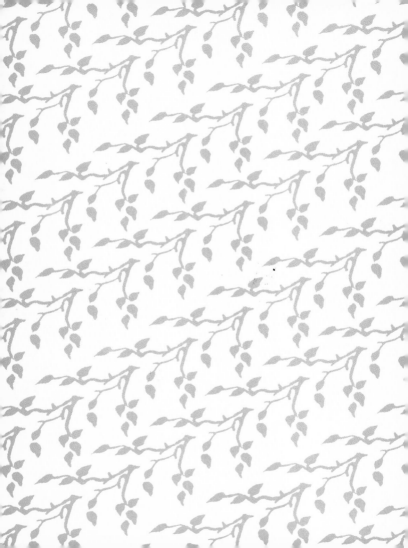